25TH ANNIVERSARY EDITION

HERSHEL
· and the ·
HANUKKAH GOBLINS
BY ERIC KIMMEL
ILLUSTRATED BY
TRINA SCHART HYMAN

HOLIDAY HOUSE · NEW YORK

To Nana
E.A.K.

For Linda Stein, with love
T.S.H.

This story first appeared in *Cricket, The Magazine for Children.*

Text copyright © 1985 by Eric A. Kimmel
Illustrations copyright © 1989 by Trina Schart Hyman
Afterword copyright © 2014 by Holiday House, Inc.
All Rights Reserved
HOLIDAY HOUSE is registered in the U.S. Patent and Trademark Office.
Printed and Bound in April 2014 at Toppan Leefung, DongGuan City, China.
www.holidayhouse.com
1 3 5 7 9 10 8 6 4 2

Library of Congress Cataloging-in-Publication Data
Kimmel, Eric A.
Hershel and the Hanukkah goblins / by Eric A. Kimmel ; illustrated by Trina Schart Hyman. —
25th anniversary edition.
pages cm
Summary: Relates how Hershel outwits the goblins that haunt the old synagogue
and prevent the village people from celebrating Hanukkah.
ISBN 978-0-8234-3164-9 (hardcover)
[1. Hanukkah—Fiction. 2. Goblins—Fiction.] I. Hyman, Trina Schart, illustrator. II. Title.
PZ7.K5648He 2014
[E]—dc23
2013048854
ISBN-13: 978-0-8234-3164-9 (hardcover)
ISBN-13: 978-0-8234-3194-6 (paperback)

It was the first night of Hanukkah. Hershel of Ostropol was walking down the road. He was tired and hungry. Nonetheless, his step was light. Soon he would reach the next village, where bright candles, merry songs, and platters piled high with tasty potato latkes awaited him.

But when he arrived, the village was silent and dark. Not a single Hanukkah candle could be seen.

"Isn't tonight the first night of Hanukkah?" Hershel asked the villagers.

"We don't have Hanukkah, Hershel," one of them answered sadly.

"No Hanukkah? How can that be?"

"It's because of the goblins. They haunt the old synagogue at the top of the hill. They hate Hanukkah. Whenever we try to light a menorah, the goblins blow out the candles. They break our dreidels. They throw our potato latkes on the floor. Those wicked goblins make our lives miserable all year long, but on Hanukkah it's really bad."

Hershel knew he must help the village people. "I'm not afraid of goblins," he said. "Tell me how to get rid of them."

"It's not as easy as you think," the rabbi warned. "You must spend eight nights in the old synagogue. The Hanukkah candles must be lit each night. On the eighth night, the king of the goblins must light them himself. That is the only way to break their power."

"I'm not afraid, Rabbi," Hershel said. "If I can't outwit a few goblins, then my name isn't Hershel of Ostropol."

The villagers wished Hershel good luck. They had no potato latkes to give him, so they packed several hard-boiled eggs for him to eat, along with a big jar of pickles. The rabbi gave Hershel a brass menorah, a package of candles, and a box of matches. Then the villagers said good-bye. Nobody expected to see Hershel again.

It was long past sundown by the time Hershel climbed to the top of the hill where the old synagogue stood. The crumbling building was gloomy and dark, and rusty hinges squealed as Hershel opened the door. Hershel shuddered. Well could he believe that goblins lived here!

He put two candles in the menorah and set it on the windowsill. He struck a match and lit the *shammes* candle. He said the blessings and was about to light the other candle when he heard a voice.

"Hey! What are you doing?"

Hershel turned around. Here was a goblin no bigger than a horsefly, with a long, pointy tail and two little bats' wings, hovering in the air.

"I'm lighting Hanukkah candles," Hershel said. "Tonight is the first night of Hanukkah."

"Oh no it's not! We don't allow Hanukkah. Not around here."

"Is that so?" said Hershel. "Who's going to stop me? A little pip-squeak like you?"

"I may be little, but I'm strong," said the goblin.

"Really? Can you crush rocks in your hand?" asked Hershel.

The goblin laughed. "Crush rocks? You're joking. Nobody's that strong!"

"I am! Watch!" Hershel took a hard-boiled egg from his pocket and squeezed it until the yolk and the white ran through his fingers. "That's how hard I'm going to squeeze you if you try to stop me from lighting these candles."

The little goblin's eyes opened wide, since in the dim light the egg looked exactly like a rock. The little goblin shook with fear. "You leave me alone," he squeaked.

"Gladly," said Hershel, "if you let me light my candles in peace."

"All right," said the goblin. "One night won't make a difference. But you better not be here tomorrow. Big, scary goblins are coming—much bigger than I! If they catch you lighting Hanukkah candles, you'll be sorry!"

"We'll see about that," Hershel said to himself. He lit the first candle.

On the second night, another goblin appeared. This one was big and fat and waddled like a goose.

Hershel was finishing his dinner of pickles and hard-boiled eggs. "Have some pickles," he said to the goblin.

"Pickles?"

"Here, catch!" Hershel tossed him a sour pickle. The goblin caught it in his mouth and swallowed it.

"*Mmmm!* Pickles are good!"

"Do you like them? I have plenty in this jar. Take all you want."

The greedy goblin grabbed as many pickles as his claws could hold, but when he tried to pull his fist out of the jar, he couldn't.

"I'm stuck!" the goblin shouted. "You put a spell on this jar to hold me fast!"

"That's right," Hershel said, laughing. "And it's a very powerful spell. You came here tonight to stop me from lighting Hanukkah candles. So now I am going to light them while you stand with your hand in that jar and watch. How do you like that?"

"No! No!" the goblin screamed. "I hate Hanukkah!"

"Too bad. You'll have to get used to it." Hershel said the blessings and lit the candles—slowly. Then he sang all his favorite Hanukkah songs. The goblin wailed and carried on so much that Hershel finally decided to let him go.

"Shall I tell you how to break the spell?"

"Yes! Yes! I can't stand it any more!"

"Let go of the pickles. Your greed is the only spell holding you prisoner."

The goblin let go of the pickles. His hand slipped out of the jar easily. How that goblin raged! He had stood with his hand in a pickle jar while Hershel lit Hanukkah candles under his nose. The furious goblin stamped his foot so hard that he shattered into a million pieces. The wind blew them away.

The third night came. Hershel felt something watching him as he set the candles in the menorah. Instead of lighting them he began playing with the dreidel. An hour passed. Hershel looked up. Sitting across the table was another goblin. This one had a fiery red face and two enormous horns. "It's getting late," the goblin said. "When are you going to light the candles?"

"Later. There's plenty of time." Hershel spun his dreidel. "This is more fun."

"What are you playing with?" the goblin asked. "It looks like a top."

"It's a dreidel. Don't you know about dreidels?"

"No."

"Too bad. Dreidels are lots of fun. You can also make lots of money if you know how to play."

"Really?" The goblin was interested now. All goblins like money. This one was no exception. "How do you play?"

"It's very simple," Hershel said. "But you must have gold. That's the first rule."

"I have plenty. Is this enough?" The goblin poured a pile of gold coins onto the table.

"That's fine," Hershel said. "Listen carefully now. This letter is *Shin*. If it comes up you give me a handful of gold. This letter is *Hay*. If it comes up you give me half your gold. This is *Gimel*. If the dreidel falls on this letter, you give me all your gold. Understand?"

"Wait. There's one letter left. What about this one?"

"That's *Nun*. If the dreidel falls on *Nun*, I don't give you anything. Ready? Let's play. You go first."

The goblin spun the dreidel. The little top whirled round and round. When it fell, the letter on top was *Shin*. "Too bad," Hershel said, taking a big handful of the goblin's gold. "Try again. Maybe you'll have better luck." The goblin spun the dreidel once more. This time it fell on *Hay*. "This isn't your night," Hershel said, helping himself to half the goblin's gold. "One more time. Your luck is bound to improve." Once again the goblin spun. This time the dreidel landed on *Gimel*. "Too bad," Hershel sighed as he took the rest of the goblin's gold. "Would you like me to spin?"

"Yes," the goblin grumbled. He was very un-happy about losing his money.

Hershel spun the dreidel. This time the letter *Nun* was on top. "Oh my! I don't give you any-thing. I get to keep all the gold. Say, that was fun! Get some more gold and we'll play again."

"What about the Hanukkah candles?"

"We'll light them later. There's plenty of time."

"Not for me!" the goblin said. "I'm leaving now. I don't like this game. I don't like Hanuk-kah, and I don't like you."

"Don't go!" Hershel pleaded. "I know lots of games. Stay awhile. We'll have fun."

"Good-bye!" The goblin spread his wings, swooped out the door, and flew off into the night. Hershel lit the candles all by himself.

On the following nights other goblins came. One had six heads. One had three eyes. All were terrible and fierce. They growled and roared and changed themselves into horrible shapes. They tried to stop Hershel from lighting the Hanukkah candles. But Hershel fooled them all.

Finally the seventh night arrived. Eight tiny candles flickered on the windowsill. Hershel sat back to enjoy their light. Where were the goblins? Had they finally given up?

Hershel felt very sleepy. His eyes closed. Suddenly, he sat up. He heard a horrible sound—a voice that sounded like the cracking of bones.

"Happy Hanukkah, Hershel of Ostropol."

"Who is it? Who's there?"

"Don't you know who I am, Hershel? Weren't you expecting...THE KING OF THE GOB-LINS?" The voice rose to a hurricane roar. It ripped the shingles from the synagogue roof and shattered the windows. The Hanukkah candles reeled in the savage blast, but they did not go out.

"You're too early!" Hershel shrieked. "You're not supposed to come until tomorrow!"

The great wind died down. "Don't worry, Her-shel. I am far away, but I have the power to see you and speak to you. Enjoy this Hanukkah evening, my friend. It will be your last! Tomor-row night I will come for you. You fooled my slaves, the other goblins. Let's see if you can fool me."

Poor Hershel! What was he to do? The king of the goblins was on his way and no power on earth could stop him. Unless...unless... Her-shel had an idea. It was a big chance, but he had to take it. It was the only way to save himself— and Hanukkah.

It was the last night of Hanukkah. Hershel set the candles in the menorah. But instead of placing it on the windowsill, he put the menorah and the box of matches on a small table near the door. Then he sat down to wait.

Night fell. It grew dark as pitch inside the gloomy old synagogue. Outside, the whole world lay cold and silent.

Suddenly a great gust ripped the synagogue door from its hinges. The whole building shook. A fearsome voice spoke.

"HERSHEL OF OSTROPOL!"

"Did I hear something?"

"IT IS I, THE KING OF THE GOBLINS!"

Hershel laughed. "Don't be silly. You're one of the boys from the village. You're trying to scare me."

"I AM NOT A BOY! I AM THE KING OF THE GOBLINS!"

"I'll believe it when I see it. Show yourself to me."

"BEHOLD! I STAND BEFORE YOU! DO YOU BELIEVE ME NOW?"

Hershel tried not to look. Even in the darkness he could see the outline of a monstrous shape filling the doorway, a figure too horrible to describe. He pretended not to care.

"It's too dark. I can't see anything. A candle-stick and some matches are by the doorway. Why don't you light a few candles? Then I'll see what you really are."

"INDEED YOU SHALL!"

A match flared. The *shammes* candle caught the flame. Hershel's blood turned to water at the awful sight before him, but he did not lose courage. "Master of the world," he silently prayed. "Thou who created the heavens and the earth and the spirits of the air, stand by me now." Then he addressed the goblin. "It's still too dark. What are you afraid of? There are plenty of candles. Why not light them all?"

A hideous hand took the *shammes* candle and lit the others one by one. Hershel felt himself growing faint, but he forced himself to look. His eyes grew wider and wider as each candle caught the flame. Six...seven...eight. The king of the goblins stood before him.

"NOW, HERSHEL, DO YOU KNOW WHO I AM?"

"I know you're not Queen Esther."

"VERY FUNNY! ENJOY THE JOKE! IT WILL BE YOUR LAST!"

"That's what you think. Begone, or I'll take a stick to you!"

"HOW DARE YOU SPEAK TO THE KING OF THE GOBLINS THAT WAY!"

"I'll speak to you any way I please. You have no power. Your spell is broken. See! The menorah is lit. You thought those were ordinary candles you were lighting. They weren't. They were Hanukkah candles. And you lit them yourself!"

The king of the goblins roared with fury. The earth trembled and a mighty wind arose. It ripped off the synagogue roof and blew down the walls. It splintered the great timbers and scattered them like matchsticks. Around the menorah the whirlwind howled, but the candles never flickered. They burned with clear, steady flames. The king of the goblins had no power over them. The spirit of Hanukkah had triumphed.

The great wind vanished as suddenly as it had risen. Hershel rubbed his eyes. The night was as still as before, even though the synagogue was gone. Walls, floor, roof—even the foundation stones had vanished. But the menorah remained, standing tall upon the little table where Hershel had placed it.

Hershel waited until the last candle burned out. Then he started down the road that led to the village. I'd better hurry, he thought. I don't want to miss the last night of Hanukkah.

But there was no reason to worry. In every window there stood a menorah with nine gleaming candles to light the way.

The whole village was waiting for him.

AFTERWORD

Hershel and the Hanukkah Goblins began as an experiment to see if I could create a Hanukkah story along the lines of Charles Dickens's *A Christmas Carol*. I started with a Ukrainian story, *Ivanko, the Bear's Son*. Ivanko fools a goblin who lives in a lake. Why not multiply that goblin eight times and use a Jewish folk character, Hershel of Ostropol, as the hero? I gave it a try and felt I'd written a good story. Unfortunately, every editor I sent it to turned it down. I eventually gave up submitting it.

Then Marianne Carus of *Cricket* magazine asked if I had a Hanukkah story for an upcoming December issue. I. B. Singer had promised to write one but wasn't going to be able to finish it on time. I found that flattering. How often is a writer asked to fill in for a Nobel prizewinner?

The problem was that I didn't have any Hanukkah stories except this one unusual tale. I told Marianne I would send it to her.

Marianne liked it. The story was published in the December 1985 issue of *Cricket* with two-color illustrations by Trina Schart Hyman. I was overcome. Although I had been introduced to Trina on a few occasions, I never imagined she would illustrate a story of mine. I was thrilled by my good fortune.

John Briggs of Holiday House can tell you the rest.

Eric A. Kimmel

Talk about thrilled . . . we adored Trina's art as much as we adored her, so as soon as we read Eric's story, we rushed to sign up the book. Our contract with Eric was the first of many in what has proven to be an especially gratifying relationship.

As soon as she finished the illustrations, Trina wrote to Eric, "I think you are a wonderful writer. One of the reasons I enjoyed working on this book—aside from the fact that it's a great story—is that you really know how to write for the artist. You, and Dylan Thomas, and Charles Dickens. You know just what to put in, and more important, what to leave out. I can't tell you what a pleasure it is to work on a manuscript that implies great visual stuff, but knows enough to stop at the implication. As a picture-book author, you're among the greats. I truly admire and appreciate your skill and professionalism, and I just wanted to say thank you for the pleasure it gave me to work on this story. . . . I think I drew him [Hershel] just right. I may have even fallen in love with him."

Eric has never forgotten the letter. "This is what she wrote to me when I was nobody from nowhere and she was one of the gods."

John Briggs